E   Kantrowitz, Mildred
K   When Violet Died

DATE DUE

APR 1 1 1978	Jo H.	
DEC 9 1980	Becky	
JAN 24 '8	Laura A.	
SEP 22 '8 LAURA		

WHEN VIOLET DIED

Written by MILDRED KANTROWITZ

Pictures by EMILY A. McCULLY

Parents' Magazine Press
New York

Library of Congress Cataloging in Publication Data

Kantrowitz, Mildred.
    When Violet died.
    SUMMARY. Saddened by her pet's death, Eva suddenly
thinks of a way to make life go on forever.
    I. McCully, Emily Arnold, illus. II. Title.
PZ7.K1285Wh   [E]   73-4384
ISBN 0-8193-0690-8, ISBN 0-7193-0691-6 (lib. bdg.)

For Fran and Bill,
Walter and Merle…and theirs

They knew that old Violet was going to die.
So it was no surprise when she did.
She left her perch on Tuesday at noon,
and lay down on her side at the bottom
of the cage.
She rested that way for the next three days.
On Friday morning Amy and Eva said good-bye
for the very last time.

The funeral was held on Saturday morning.
Close friends and neighbors were invited.
Billy came. He brought the box.
Elizabeth came to the funeral too.
She brought a ribbon to tie around the box.
She also brought her little brother Danny.
They were very dear and old friends
of the bird.

Billy, Elizabeth, Danny and Eva gathered
around and watched Amy as she placed
Violet on a bed of cotton balls, in the small,
white box.

They planted the bird and some cornflower seeds
in the corner of the garden, next to the lilac bush.
It was a simple ceremony.

"We will now have entertainment," Amy announced.
"First I will read the poem that I wrote,
Then Eva will sing. Then..."
"Count me out!" said Billy, waving good-bye.
"I just remembered I have a terrible stomachache."

"Oh that's too bad," said Eva.

"Amy made some strawberry punch."

Billy paused.

"…with real strawberries," Amy added.

Billy stayed.

He suddenly felt much better.

Amy read her poem:

Vi-o-let, dear Vi-o-let,
If you could only see
How sad I am that you are gone,
You'd fly right back to me.

"That's gorgeous," said Elizabeth.
"I could cry, it's so gorgeous."

Danny and Eva applauded.

Billy groaned.

"This is a very boring funeral," he said.

"Next on our program," announced Amy,
"will be a song. A bird song."

Eva stepped to the front. She cleared her throat.
"Excuse me," she said. "I'm a little hoarse…"
"Funny you don't look like one," shouted Billy.
"But I bet you sound just like one!
Get it? A little HORSE! Ha—ha!"

"Sing, Eva," said Amy.

Eva sang:

*When the red, red robin
comes bob, bob, bobbin'
along, along...
When the red, red robin
comes bob, bob, bobbin'
along.*

Punch was served. Billy was happy at last.
The guests departed.

Amy and Eva walked back to the house.
"It was such a beautiful funeral.
Violet would have loved it.
I'm sorry she wasn't there," said Amy.
"I'M sorry she WAS!" said Eva.

The cage hung empty in the dining room.
Amy just couldn't bear to look.
Eva bent down to pet the big, white cat
that rubbed up against her leg.
"We still have Blanche," she said. "Forever and ever."
"Nothing lasts forever…nothing," said Amy sadly.
She went upstairs to her room.

The cat followed Eva into the kitchen.

Soon she would have her kittens.

Any day now.

Eva poured some milk into the bowl.

When Blanche has her kittens, she thought,

I will keep one, and I will call the kitten Blanche...

And when that Blanche grows up,

SHE will have kittens...

and I will keep one of hers...

and I will name HER Blanche...

and SHE will grow up and have kittens...

and I will keep one and

name HER Blanche and...

Eva was all excited.
She ran up the stairs to tell Amy...
that maybe nothing lasts forever,
but she knew a way to make it
last a long, long time!

Mildred Kantrowitz studied painting and sculpture and was working as a book designer when she became interested in writing for children. Her first picture book, *Maxie*, was selected as one of the best books of the year, 1970, by the *School Library Journal* and has since been published in several foreign countries. She is also the author of *I Wonder if Herbie's Home Yet* and *Good-bye, Kitchen*. (All of the above are published by Parents' Magazine Press.)

Emily A. McCully was awarded a gold medal by the Philadelphia Art Directors Club in 1968, and since then she has illustrated many popular books for children including *Hurray for Captain Jane! Maxie* and *The Mouse and the Elephant*, all three for Parents' Magazine Press. Mrs. McCully was born in Illinois and graduated from Pembroke College of Brown University. She received her M.A. in Art History at Columbia.